Reflections of Fear

Created by Joe Duncombe

Illustrated by Cong Nguyen

Published by Flat Basset Publishing

Matchbox

Wooden beams turn cinder,
dark ash covers my hair.
The screaming stopped some time ago.
I dropped my matchbox somewhere.

CREAK!!

The Creak in my Floor

My daughter went up the stairs,
and the floor did creak.

My wife went up the stairs,
and the floor did creak.

I went up the stairs,
and the floor did creak...

And the floor did creak.

Haiku of the Dead

Leaves fall from the trees...
Men and women stay inside;
Cars lay still in road.

Snow blankets city,
footprints, barely interrupt...
Am I all alone?

Marigolds flower;
Grand old buildings crumble down...
Dead men walk again.

The sun heats the ground;
putrid smell carries on air...
Arm is sore from bite.

The Gardener

At the back of a house,
as some people know.
A man tends to his garden,
where his flowers did grow.

His Rose's were red,
and his Daisy's were mauve.
The colours were plentiful,
where his flowers did grow.

People would travel,
from around the globe,
to take in the beauty,
where his flowers did grow.

The man got great joy,
when his garden did show,
all of it's wonders,
where his flowers did grow.

The crowds would ask,
for his secrets to flow,
about his beautiful garden,
where his flowers did grow.

He would not tell them,
or let anyone know;
about the pretty young women,
where his flowers did grow.

The young girl would see,
when the moon did glow,
the mystical beauty,
where his flowers did grow.

And once he had them,
all tied in a bow,
he would brutally kill them,
where his flowers did grow.

He would carefully place them,
so that their blood would flow,
all over the garden,
where his flowers did grow.

But on one of these nights,
with a girl in tow.
His garden would change,
where his flowers did grow.

To the back of his head,
she dealt him a blow,
and he fell to the floor,
where his flowers did grow.

The plants withered and died,
as his body did so.
Gone was the garden,
where his flowers did grow.

Sally's Eyes

Stood by the bed,
caressing his cheek.
As he lay dead still.
She toyed, with the knife and his health.

Mesmerised by
his big baby blues.
Lovingly, she said
"Your eyes would look good, on my
shelf."

A Skeleton in the Closet

There's a skeleton in my closet,
he's been hanging there all day.
There's a skeleton in my closet,
He's been waiting just to say.

"Why do you keep me locked here?
was killing me not enough?
Please, do stop this torture!
my bones are not so tough."

The Girl That Has No Teeth

Mary's smile was magical,
it infected others once seen;
the white pearls of her mouth,
were glorious in how they screamed.

One night in her bathroom,
ivory fell in the sink.
Mary would smile, nevermore.
She was now, the girl with no teeth.

Don't go in the Woods

Don't go into the woods,
But if you do go in pairs.
There's something in those woods,
but don't be scared of the bears.

If you decide please take care,
not to go too deep.
Open your eyes and keep to the path,
as something there does creep.

Your heart will beat fast and your breath
get heavy,
as your fear does thrive.
When it's too late and you're fully aware,
That these trees are alive.

The Porcelain Doll

It's not her cold, dark eyes
that concerns me.
It's how she watches the hall.

And it's not, how she sits
that concerns me.
It's how she starts to crawl.

The Stranger

I could hear the thunder loud
and the rain hit the roof.
But I wasn't quite safe;
with a drink in the old crooked bar.

I kept my head down low
and I stayed to myself.
I felt empty in there;
as I nursed the swill in my glass.

The door crashed open and wide
but I never looked up.
Sounds of boots cross the floor;
he ordered a bottle of brown.

My stillness was broken,
I was forced to converse.
"May I sit with you here?"
I nodded my affirmation.

The stranger sat with me
and filled up our glasses.
"How's the day been for you?"
And I answered, with a hard grunt.

He began to regale me
with what, I didn't hear.
My mind started swirling,
with vile demons laughing at me.

The were dancing with joy
and they tortured my soul.
I was bondage in hell,
with cackling imps in dominion.

I'd almost forgotten
that I wasn't alone,
the piano came to life,
and played the most dire of dirge.

My head watered with sweat
and my heart beat in pain.
The stranger voiced concern,
"Bartholomew, are you okay?"

I looked up at his face
for the first time tonight.
His eyes were pale and deep.
I asked, "How do you know my name?"

He grinned with yellow teeth,
"I know all about you."
Fear gripped my insides.
I wondered, "With whom do I drink?"

He leant closer to me
to whisper while I sat.
"Your soul's on the line, as
tonight, you drink with the devil."

The Duality of Fey

Fairies.
Kind, playful,
helping, dancing, flitting.
Beware the duality of the fey.
Undying, dominating, hindering,
grim, cruel.
Fairies.

Ghost House Sestina

If you come to this house at night
beware, the air will go cold.
Inside this house is dark,
so be careful, if you run.
This house is home to a spirit;
be wary of tricks to your head.

If clouds appear in your head
as if it's a stormy night,
it maybe some kind of spirit.
If the room starts to go cold
listen, the wind begins to run
and the light turns to dark.

Evil creeps in the dark
and it wants to take your head;
it wants your blood to run.
You won't survive the night.
And your body will slowly go cold,
just another victim of the spirit.

You may never see the spirit,
as you stand alone in the dark
which is as black, as the winter is cold.
"Finally," you think in your head,
"I'm safe till the end of the night."
And you forget, that you shouldn't run.

But as certain as a stream does run,
a vision appears of the spirit.
And in the loneliness of night
your sight, will fade to dark...
Because the ghost has take your head,
and your skin is going cold.

The blood is warm not cold
and across the floor does run...
as the body, is missing its head.
Your breath floats away with your spirit
which lurks forever in dark,
screaming into the night.

If your house is cold and a spirit harbours there,
you should run before going inside, or you'll
meet dark embrace.
Heed this advice to keep your head and be ever
fearful, of the night.

The Living Doll Show

If you go to the show tonight,
be ready for marvel and joy.
But be prepared for quite a fright,
when fair maidens are turned to toy.

If you take in the show this night,
your mind may build with fear.
When your legs want to take flight
stay seated, you're better off here.

If you watch the show this eve
you'll leave, dripping in sin.
For these girls you may want to grieve,
as I begin, to flail their skin.

The show this evening does contain
scenes with plenty of gore.
Your clothes, this resin will not stain,
which over her body I slowly pour.

We approach the end of our show for
now,
so to her arms I'll attach some rope.
With pulleys, she'll dance and take a bow,
and live forever on stage I hope.

So if you enjoyed the show tonight
and to your nerves, it didn't take a toll.
Tell your friends of the wonderful sight,
of my beautiful, living doll.

Will I Turn Tonight?

The dark of the night;
punctured by spots of stars.
I look for the luminous moon,
as I anticipate it's shape.

The nerves of my skin
thunder into life
and I smell the sweet scent of a rabbit;
upon the wind carried afar.

Dreams of running free,
through trees and grassy fields
dirt scatters on my legs;
and warm blood fills my mouth.

Will I turn tonight?
A question I ask all the time.
And when my hair and teeth do grow
I know, my primal wolf is here to play.

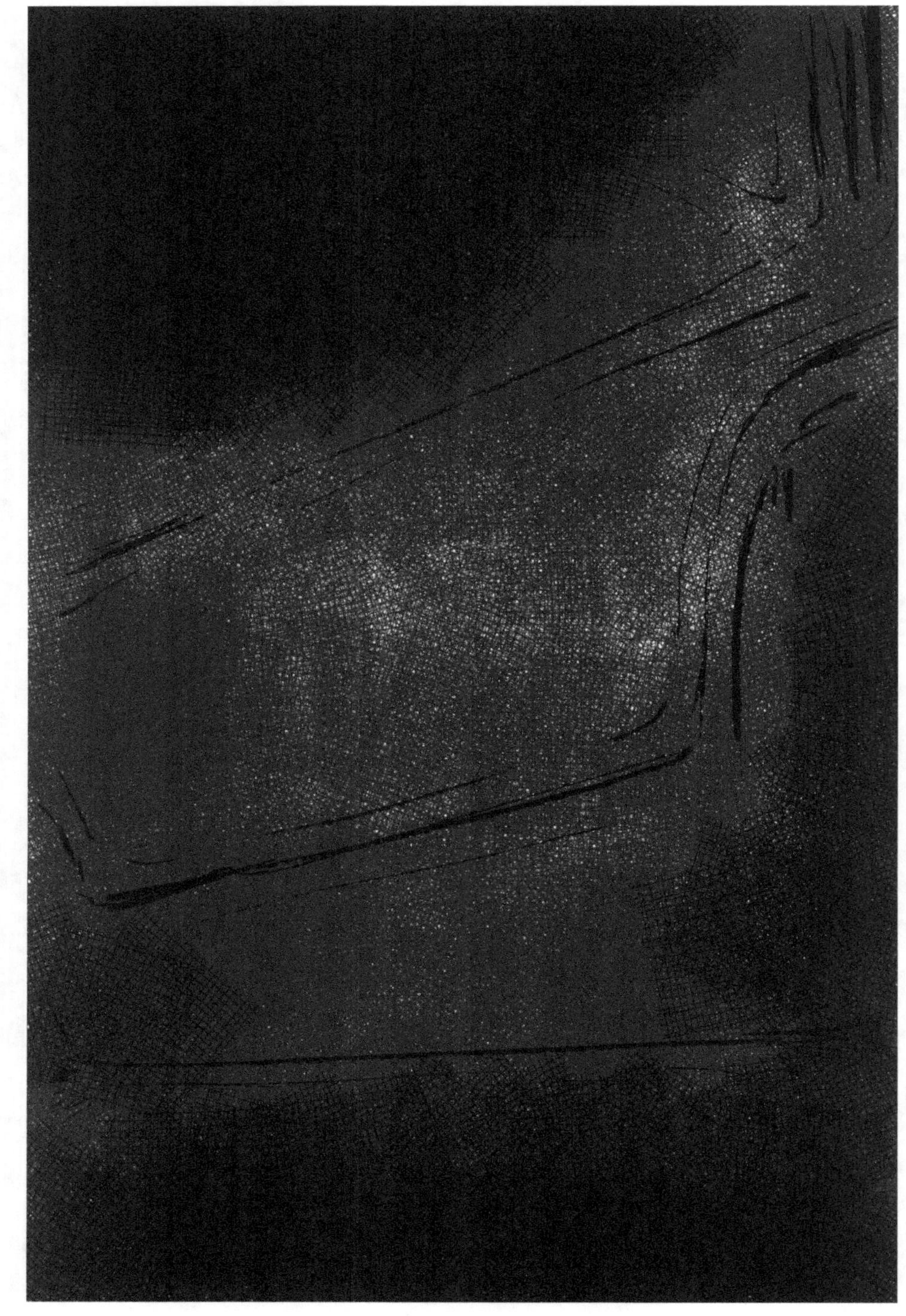

The Long Dark Ride

The sound of the radio;
muffled show-tunes play.
I can't make out the music,
or the words that they say.

Cable ties my hands.
I struggle against my bonds.
My body bumps on the side.
I wonder who I wronged.

Travel has come to an end,
the sound of life comes to a stop.
My heart beats with high tempo
yet my body's, still like a prop.

The fumble of keys outside.
Will someone please let me out?
I look up at the sound of a click,
all I can do is muffle a shout.

The hatch opens in due time,
the light is blinding to see.
I can make out the outline of a man
with a shovel, smiling at me.

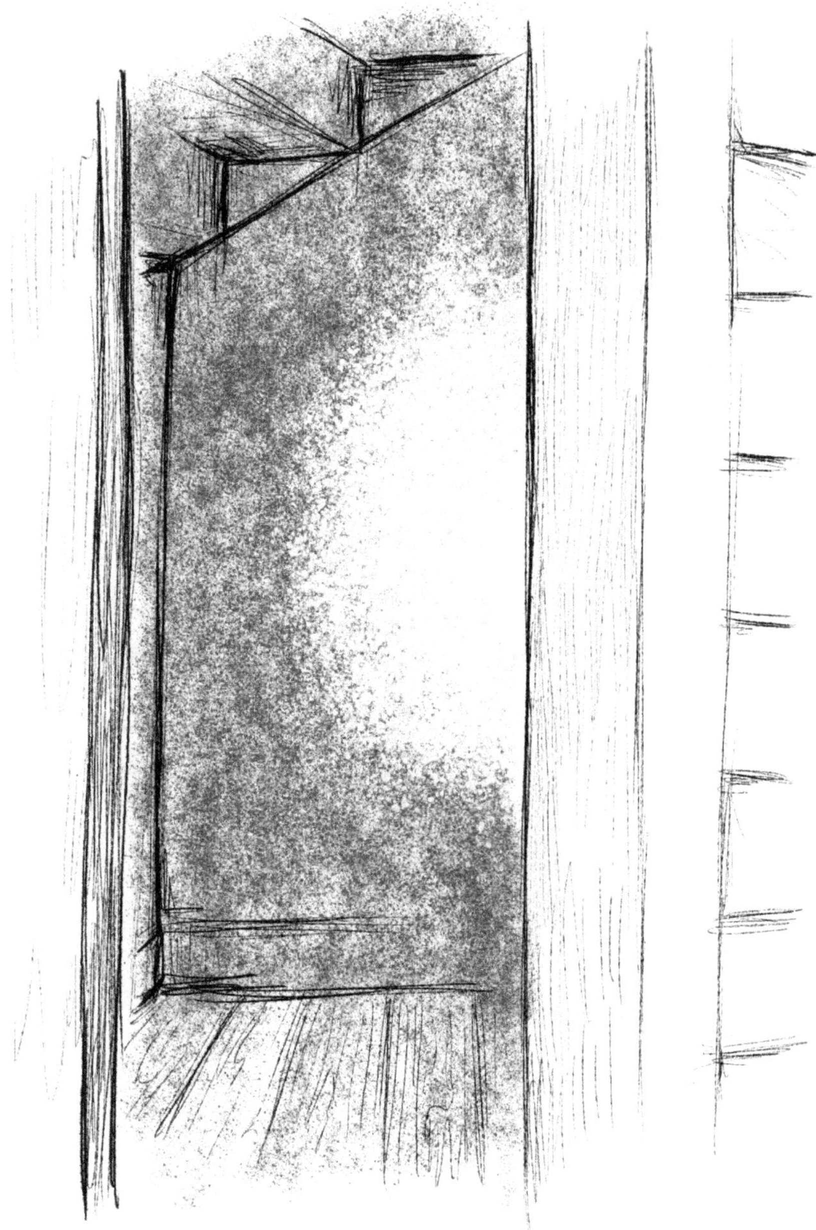

The Lost Cupboard of Dreams

There's a cupboard under my stairs.
It used to be cluttered,
with memories and dreams.

One day, the back wall opened into a
perilous void
and like a giant black hole, nothing
escaped it's pull.

I stay away from that door now, it's not
been open in months.
And now my cupboard of memory and
dreams sits...
empty.

The Mirror Man

Every morning,
I look at the mirror
and as I straighten my tie
I, never feel quite right.

My wearied face,
it's never shown to me
but the mirror man instead
smiles, and gleefully winks.

Every evening,
I look out from the mirror
and as he takes off his tie
I, think of what he has done.

He takes my hand,
and tomorrow I know,
that when I look at the glass the mirror man
will once again, take my place.

Descent

Her slow descent
begun with sudden impact.
She looked toward
where ripples had once been formed.
Nothing is seen,
no light breaks through her surround.
Pushed from behind,
who started her journey down?
Fall forever.
Does this abyss have a ground?

My Clay Mask

I wear a mask of clay.
I've worn it everyday.
I struggle to find a way,
as the veil hides what I try to say.

What Piper must I pay?
To lift the mask that lay.
But my world remains still grey,
as forever this mask shall stay.